Mim's Christmas Jam

ANDREA DAVIS PINKNEY

Illustrated by BRIAN PINKNEY

Gulliver Books

Harcourt, Inc.

San Diego   New York   London

For Aunt Elsie
—A. D. P.

For Shelly Fogelman
—B. P.

Many thanks to the New York City Transit Museum,
and to recipe expert Diane Vezza, for testing and perfecting Mim's jam recipe
—A. D. P.

Gulliver Books is a trademark of Harcourt, Inc., registered
in the United States of America and/or other jurisdictions.

Library of Congress Cataloging-in-Publication Data
Pinkney, Andrea Davis.
Mim's Christmas jam/Andrea Davis Pinkney; Brian Pinkney, illustrator.
p. cm.
"Gulliver Books."
Summary: When Pap goes away to build the New York City subway in 1915, his family sends him Mother's
special jam which works magic in returning him home to celebrate Christmas.
1. Afro-Americans—Juvenile fiction. [1. Afro-Americans—Fiction. 2. Christmas—Fiction.
3. Family life—Fiction. 4. Subways—New York (State)—New York—Fiction.]
I. Pinkney, J. Brian, ill. II. Title.
PZ7.P6333Mi 2001
[E]—dc21 99-6346
ISBN 0-15-201918-9

First edition
A C E G H F D B
Manufactured in China

The illustrations in this book were done with luma dyes and acrylic on scratchboard.
The display type was set in Nutcracker.
The text type was set in Sabon.
Color separations by Bright Arts Ltd., Hong Kong
Manufactured by South China Printing Company, Ltd., China
This book was printed on totally chlorine-free Nymolla Matte Art paper.
Production supervision by Sandra Grebenar and Ginger Boyer
Designed by Lydia D'moch

Drillin', Poundin', Blastin'—Building

Construction of the New York City subway system began in 1900 and the first major phase was completed in 1925. During this period more than thirty thousand men found employment building the underground railway network. This workforce consisted mostly of African Americans and Italian and Irish immigrants—men eager for the chance to earn a steady living despite the risks and the drudgery involved.

Subway laborers faced dangerous conditions. Dynamite explosions, cave-ins, and tunnels collapsing underwater were a few of the hazards that came with the job. Many workers were injured; some died. A subway worker's family often faced the possibility of losing a brother, a husband, a father, or a friend to the perils that lurked at each dig site. Those who stood up to the toilsome work contributed greatly to a system that continues to be New York's leading mode of transportation.

Today nearly four million people ride the subway each weekday. It has been hailed as an engineering marvel. *Under the Sidewalks of New York: The Story of the Greatest Subway System in the World* (Fordham University Press, 1995) by Brian J. Cudahy gives a full account of the subway's origins and construction.

Every Christmas season Pap bundled up Saraleen and Royce and took them to chop down the biggest tree they could find on their plot of land called Wildroot.

No matter how far they went, Pap claimed he could smell Mim's belly-hum jam bubbling on the stove. Belly-hum was Mim's specialty jam, which she made to serve with Christmas Eve dinner. Pap would take a big sniff and say, "There ain't nothin' like a batch of belly-hum." Then he'd start whistling a deep hooty tune. Mim's jam had a way of doing that to people.

But this year, 1915, was different. Pap was off in New York City, digging a long, wide hole for something called the *subway*. The holiday season wasn't the same without Pap. It was plain miserable. No tree. No whistling. No fun.

"If Pap was here in Pennsylvania, we'd be searching Wildroot for the biggest tree this side of Scranton," Royce whined.

"But he *ain't* here," Saraleen said.

Mim hugged her children tightly. "We still got my belly-hum," she reminded them. "And we can still decorate, even though we don't have a tree. Let's make a batch of belly-hum for Pap. Spruce it up real nice, like a present from the mercantile."

"The recipe for belly-hum has been in my family since slave time," Mim told her children. "Lots of other folk have tried their hand at belly-hum. Nobody but my very own blood-kin can give the jam the special thing that makes it sing inside your belly. Family pride and the love we have for one another are the main ingredients."

When the jam was just right, Mim sealed the jar tightly with wax and a square of muslin. Saraleen wrapped up a spoon in the comics page of the *Trixton Register*. Royce decorated the jar with a sprig of pine. Then they sent the jam to Pap.

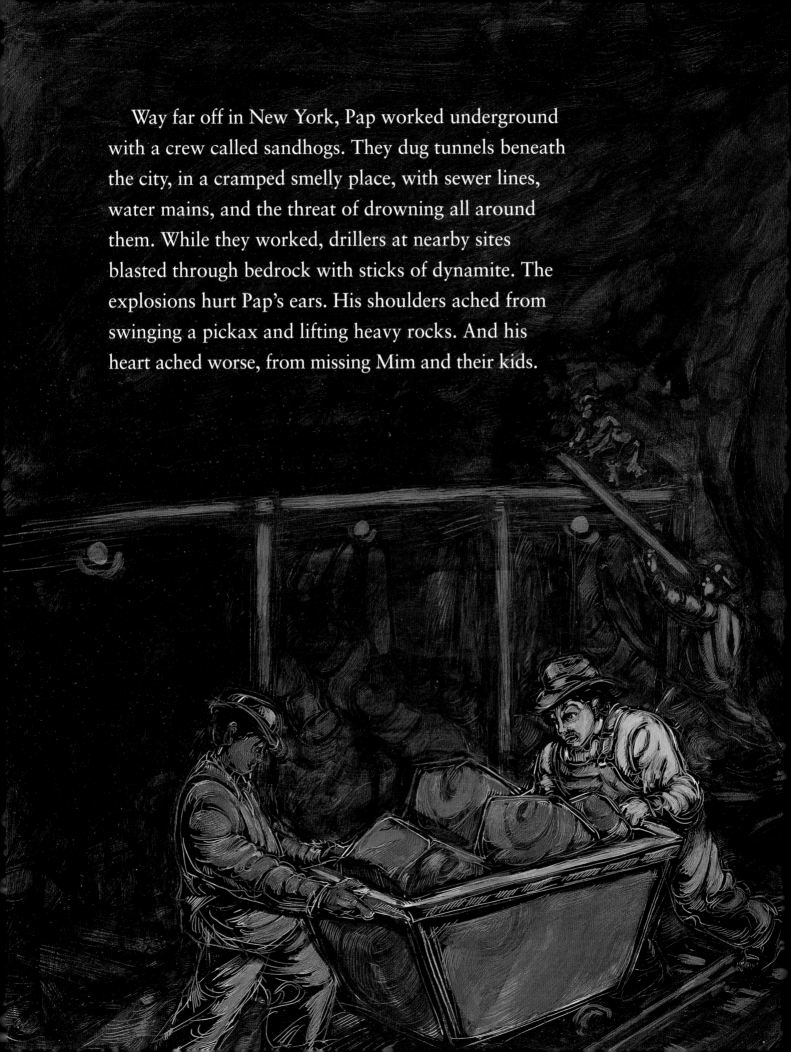

Way far off in New York, Pap worked underground
with a crew called sandhogs. They dug tunnels beneath
the city, in a cramped smelly place, with sewer lines,
water mains, and the threat of drowning all around
them. While they worked, drillers at nearby sites
blasted through bedrock with sticks of dynamite. The
explosions hurt Pap's ears. His shoulders ached from
swinging a pickax and lifting heavy rocks. And his
heart ached worse, from missing Mim and their kids.

The workers called the dig site's two bossy foremen—
Mr. Mead and Mr. Evans—Mean and Evil. Every day,
all day, Mean and Evil yelled: *"Keep drillin', keep*
poundin', keep pickin' and haulin'...Keep blastin',
keep loadin', keep sweatin', keep crawlin'!"

One day, as Christmas drew closer, Pap and
his friends Donovan, Gilletti, and Jones began
to sing carols to make their work go faster,
and to ease the pain of being separated from
their families.

When Mean and Evil heard the sandhogs
singing, they hollered, "Ain't no time for
holiday crooning and soft-souled sentiment.
For every minute you men have wasted, you'll
be diggin' and haulin' on Christmas Day.
Now get back to work!"

That evening the bustling holiday shoppers made Pap miss the laughter and good times of Wildroot's holiday season even more. And he sure missed Mim's belly-hum jam. There wasn't one bit of warmth in digging a hole. Not an iota of fun in steel and stone. Pap wanted to go home, but his family needed the money he was earning. And now he wasn't even going to have a rest on Christmas Day.

Then, on Christmas Eve, a strange thing happened. The jar of belly-hum from Mim and the children arrived. Pap whistled as he carried the jam to share with his friends. But when he offered it, his friends refused.

"You better put that stuff away," they warned. "If Mean and Evil catch us, we'll be bringin' in the holiday with twenty extra verses of *'drillin', haulin', blastin', and crawlin'.'*"

As soon as the men spoke, Mr. Mead and Mr. Evans came around to inspect. "What's going on here?" Mean snarled.

The foremen wore some serious frowns. But something had melted Pap's fear of Mr. Mead and Mr. Evans. He put a firm grip on the jam jar's lid and opened it with one twist. The delicious smell of Mim's belly-hum filled the cold tunnel. "This is from Mim and our young 'uns—best jam you'll ever eat. Belly-hum jam, Mim calls it."

Pap leaned in toward them both. "I know you two aren't much for holiday spirits. But here, take a small taste of jam."

Mr. Mead glanced at Mr. Evans. Mr. Evans looked at Pap like he'd gone sick in the head.

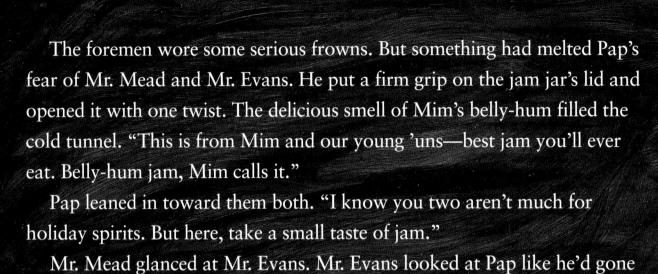

Mr. Mead said, "How dare you even *think* of chowing down on jam?"

Mr. Evans grumbled, "You're achin' for a breakin', man."

But Mim's belly-hum sure smelled fine. Mr. Evans nudged Mr. Mead. "How 'bout we take just a teeny taste?" he whispered.

"We can't waste no time samplin' sweets. We got work to do," Mr. Mead growled.

Before Mr. Mead could say another word, Mr. Evans plunged his finger into the jar and shoved a hunk of jam into his mouth. Mr. Mead's jaw dropped open. Then he followed the same way—no spoon, just his finger. "Look at that fool trying to butter up the bosses," Gilletti whispered.

"Ain't no butter in them two. They're harder than the steel girders that keep this tunnel from caving in," said Donovan.

Jones sighed. "Mean and Evil will work us till we're mincemeat."

Pap watched and waited. The foremen were silent for a long moment.

Finally both foremen let out a slow groan. "That there is some tasty jam," Mr. Evans said.

Mr. Mead just nodded. He was too busy smacking his lips to speak.

Then Mr. Mead and Mr. Evans smiled at the same time. Nobody had ever seen them smile.

Mr. Evans looked over at the busy crew. "Hey, you men!" he shouted. "Stop that! Stop it right now, I say! This dig site is closed! Closed for Christmas!"

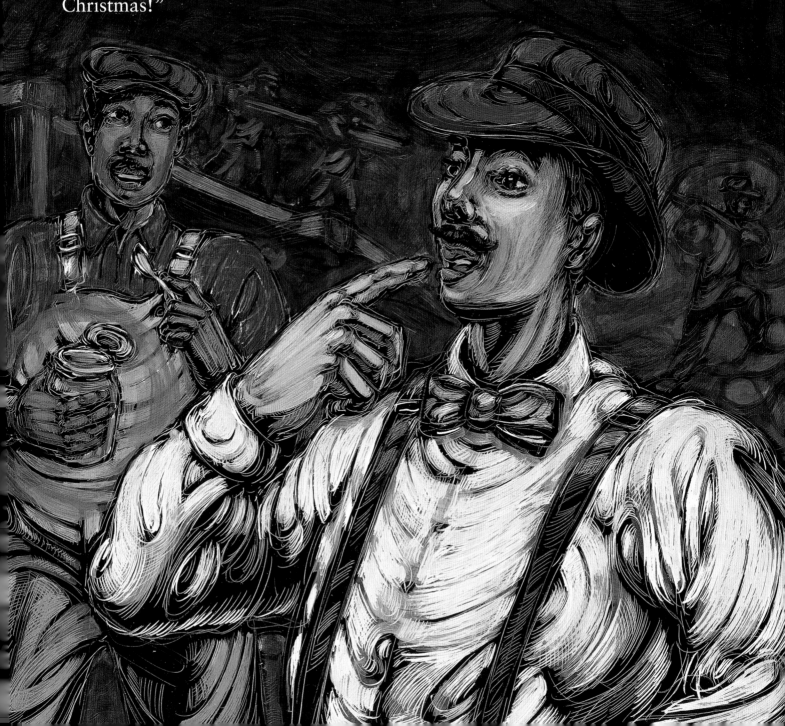

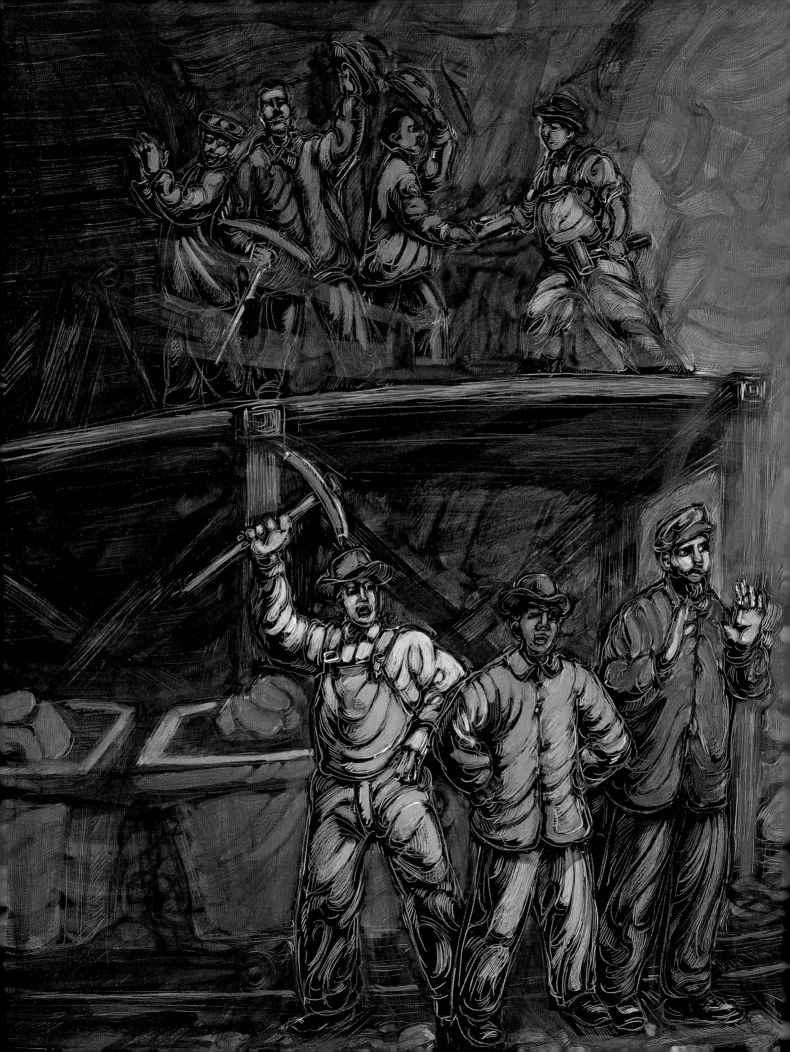

At first the men couldn't believe what they were hearing. They kept on working. But Mr. Mead called out, "*Quit drillin', quit poundin', quit pickin' and haulin'…Quit blastin', quit loadin', quit sweatin', quit crawlin'!*"

One by one the men stopped. First the chiselers set down their picks. Then the sandhogs laid their shovels and pickaxes to rest. And finally the rock men, who'd cleared mounds of dirt, put down their rusty buckets.

Everyone in the tunnel fell silent. Then Mr. Mead said softly, "Merry Christmas, men."

Pap gave his jar of belly-hum to the foremen. "Merry Christmas to you, too," he said.

Back at Wildroot, Mim and the children were singing a Christmas Eve hymn by the fire. Outside, a hooty whistle flew forward. It came quietly at first, then louder and closer.

"Saraleen, you hear that?" Royce asked. "Sounds like Pap's whistle."

"That just couldn't be," said Saraleen. "Must be an owl."

Mim was listening hard. She shushed Royce and Saraleen. "That's no owl," she said.

Soon the hooty whistle had heavy footsteps with it. Mim threw open the window. Royce called out, "*Pap?* Pap, is that you?"

And right then a voice sprang out from the night. "Mim, Royce, Saraleen—I'm home."

It *was* Pap! He was with his friends, who had a blue pine, big as a bridge, slung over their shoulders.

"This is Gilletti, Donovan, and Jones!" Pap called. "They've come to share Christmas Eve dinner, and to sample Mim's belly-hum."

That night, as Christmas settled up to Wildroot, Mim spread a prayer
of thanks for Pap's return and for the gift belly-hum had brought.
Then everyone shared in the fun of decorating the tree, and the joy of
Christmas Eve dinner.

Mim's Belly-Hum Jam

Mim's jam is easy to make but takes three to four hours to prepare.
Try a batch, and see if it puts a hum in your belly.

INGREDIENTS

- 4 pounds apples (McIntosh or Rome Beauties work best)
- 2 cups water
- granulated sugar (see step 5 for measure)
- ground cinnamon (see step 5 for measure)
- ground nutmeg, optional (see step 5 for measure)
- 1 teaspoon grated lemon peel

Have handy: five ½-pint jars with lids, melted paraffin

1. Wash jars in soapy water. Rinse them and put them in a large pot. Cover them with water and bring slowly to a boil. Carefully remove the sterilized jars with tongs. Set aside, upside down, on clean towel to dry.

2. Melt paraffin in a double boiler; keep warm.

3. Wash, core, and slice apples into a large pot; add water and bring to a boil. Cook over low heat 15 minutes, or until fruit is soft. Remove from heat and pour through a strainer or large sieve, lined with several layers of cheesecloth, into clean container.

4. Reserve ½ to 1 cup of apple mixture from strainer or sieve. Set mixture aside to cool. When cool, carefully remove any apple skin from reserved mixture.

5. Allow juice to continue to drip into container, pressing lightly with the back of a spoon against the fruit until all liquid is released. Measure juice, then return it to the pot. Add ¾ cup sugar, ½ teaspoon ground cinnamon, and a pinch of nutmeg (optional) for every cup of juice. Stir in the reserved apple mixture and grated lemon peel.

6. Cook apple mixture and juice over low heat, stirring occasionally until the sugar is dissolved. Increase heat and boil rapidly until it thickens. Skim surface. Pour the jam into sterilized jars immediately, while still warm.

7. Cover the jars with a cloth until the jam has cooled, then top each jar with two thin layers of melted paraffin. Seal the jars tightly with their lids.

   Makes five half-pint jars of jam.